(Original title: The Disappearance of Mr. Allen)

Mystery on Outer Island

by FOSTER KENNEDY

illustrated by BILL RUSSELL

SCHOLASTIC INC.

NEW YORK · TORONTO · LONDON · AUCKLAND · SYDNEY · TOKYO

For Mary Kennedy, my sister,
to thank her for her warm interest
in the writing of this book
and especially
for her belief in it.

ISBN 0-590-11841-2

Text copyright © 1977 by Foster Kennedy. Illustrations copyright © 1977 by Scholastic Magazines, Inc. All rights reserved. Published by Scholastic Inc.

12 11 10 9 8 7 6 5 4 3 2 1   3 4 5/8

Printed in the U.S.A.   01

Contents

The Vault
in the Woods

Roy ran up the slope after a young rabbit. He had a stick in his hand, and as the rabbit disappeared in the thick green growth, I saw Roy using the stick to feel around in the bushes. I heard the stick strike against something hard. When he pushed the stick, it slipped on a flat surface.

He called, "Hey fellows, come up here."

We were already at his heels. The four of us had come to camp on Center Island. We often came here. No one lived on the island. It was just across the narrow sound from Outer Island where we lived in a small settlement between the sound and the ocean. It was called East Edge.

"It's stone. It looks like a slab of coquina," said Bill. He began to clear away the vines that grew over it so that we could see it better.

"I can cut back these palmetto fans," I said, getting my hatchet. Terry helped and we cut back the ones that grew over the side. A big lizard wriggled off and scuttled away. Then we helped Roy and Bill, who had begun digging around the edge of the stone. "Lend me your hatchet, Larry." I gave it to Roy and he cut away some roots.

The stone was four or more inches deep, and we soon saw that it was set on another upright slab. The top one was about as long as my outstretched arms and about half as wide.

"This could be a vault," said Terry.

"Or a child's grave," said Bill.

"It seems funny that in all the time

we've been camping here we never noticed it before," I said. "It's all because Roy was chasing that little rabbit."

We often tried to catch a small animal for Willie Parker, the postmaster's little boy. He was always so pleased and happy over a young possum or squirrel that we sometimes went out of our way to find one. He treated it tenderly, but his father would only let him keep it for a day or two. Then he had to turn it loose.

"The rabbit ran right over this stone," said Roy.

We kept on digging. Whatever it was, it had four sides and a top. We were so excited that we decided then that before we started messing around too much we would go and tell Mr. Allan.

Mr. Allan was our teacher in East Edge and he had come back for the second year to teach us. He was interested in seeing what the islands were like and we often went with him because we knew all the islands. He told us how to look for Indian relics, and all that, and how to be careful when we discovered anything. He said we should dig with our hands, disturb nothing around it, and always to tell him if we found anything.

We never found much, some beads, a few arrowheads. Bill had unearthed an old pottery jug near an Indian mound. Mr. Allan said it might have been left by Spanish sailors. "Pirates?" we asked, and he said, "Yes, perhaps pirates." The pitcher was put on a shelf in the schoolhouse. He had a lot of respect for old things.

Mr. Allan certainly was a wonderful guy, so right away we wanted to tell him about this. We began to cover the stone slabs again with sticks and leaves.

"Look at this," Terry said.

Then we saw that there were letters cut into the top under a coat of arms.

They were worn by weather and time but we could see that the words were in a strange language.

We left our gear wrapped in a piece of oilskin near the camping site on the ridge, since we were coming right back, and scrambled down to the sand dunes where we had beached our boat.

We took turns rowing. We had been longer than we thought working around the slab and the afternoon was passing.

"All because of a little rabbit," said Roy.

"What about meeting the Walkers just when we got to the island today?" asked Bill.

"What about it?" asked Roy. He was pulling sandspurs off his clothes.

"That's right," I said. "If Slim hadn't put us down at the wrong place, Roy wouldn't have gone up that way."

"That's it," said Bill. "It was fate. That's what my pa would say. After all, there is almost never anybody on that island — and then we meet the Walkers. All very strange."

It was strange. No sooner had we come to the trail that runs the length of the island than we met Mr. Walker and his three sons: two on horseback, and Slim, the lanky youngest — he was almost thirteen, driving the two gray mules hitched to the wagon. They were followed by a pack of dogs.

The Walkers lived on Big Island across a pretty stream called Magnolia Inlet. They had a little homemade ferry, and some rowboats for crossing. They sometimes used the corral on Center Island for livestock, but we almost never ran into them. Mr. Walker was a strong, quick-moving man, more than six feet tall, with a rugged face and sharp brown eyes. He was impulsive and generous, but a man would think twice about getting into an argument with him. The two boys on horseback were older than we were, big, sun-burned, and bold. Slim was our friend.

As soon as Mr. Walker saw us he called, "Hi, fellows, can we give you a lift?"

Slim didn't slow down the wagon for us, so we ran and caught up with it. We had ridden the short distance under enormous oaks with long gray moss trailing from them, and in the under-brush was every sort of bush and pal-metto. In the marsh along the inner edge, grasses were almost over a man's head.

I had told Slim I'd show him where to put us down, but he had stopped the wagon beyond the place. We said it didn't make any difference, but thinking it over later I saw that those few yards may have made all the difference. Something began on that Saturday afternoon that would be many days unwinding. We couldn't have guessed that we would ever be involved in anything that would

be of concern to both sides of the ocean.
Even the Walkers would have a part in
it. But we didn't know any of that as we
rowed across the sound.

When we reached East Edge we
headed for Mr. Allan's dock at the south

edge of our settlement. His dock sticks out into a small cove, a beautiful spot. When we landed there we ran up to his house so fast that we were out of breath. He was outside working on a casting net. We all started talking at once.

He said, "Wait a minute, wait a minute. What's it all about?"

We told him what we had found, and he said, "That's wonderful!"

We said, "We'll show you. Let's go over there now."

But he said, "Oh no, not yet. It's a little late. The sun is almost down."

We pointed out that we had two hours before it would get really dark, but he said, "That's the trouble. We can't work on a thing like that in the dark. We'll go over there tomorrow morning."

We began guessing what the slab could be, and he joined in. "Well, it could be a gun mount, it could be part

of an old building, it could be a grave
. . . it could be just anything." So we
talked and talked until he said, "You
fellows had better go home now and
have some supper." So we left.

"We'll be around in the morning
raring to go," Bill said.

"Ready to go." Mr. Allan smiled.

Next morning as early as we could
manage we raced down the sandy road
to Mr. Allan's house — past Mr. Parker's
General Store and Post Office, past the
frame houses scattered along the way,
each with its yard, some with flowers,
some with nets drying. We spoke to
everyone we saw and answered any
who called to us from yard or porch as
we went by.

Then Roy had to chase his sister Nan
back home. She wanted to come along
with us, but we told her we had business
to attend to. She asked what kind of

business, but anyway Roy chased her home.

The small white schoolhouse had been built a little off the road in a cluster of cabbage palms. Just beyond it was Mr. Allan's house.

We were in high spirits, for who could tell what might be hidden under that coquina slab on the next island?

When we came to Mr. Allan's house it was all shut up. The shutters were down, the door was locked. There was a big padlock on it. We ran down to the dock, and his boat, the *Wandering Star*, was gone. We went back up to the house and Bill said, "Gee, his casting net is gone." We looked around and the place was bare. Everything had been taken down and put away. It certainly looked strange.

We ran back all the way to the dock where the shrimp boats come in, and where everyone had to go to get gasoline.

We were sure we'd find Mr. Allan there, loading up with gas for his motor, or laying in supplies for the day. He wasn't around anywhere. We asked one of the men on a shrimp boat if he had seen Mr. Allan, but no, he hadn't seen him. We asked two or three others, but no one had seen him.

Then we thought maybe he had gone on over to the island. We looked across the water from Bill's upstairs porch but we couldn't see the *Wandering Star* anywhere on the sound, or near the creek, or along the shore of Center Island anywhere.

We wondered what to do.

Mr. Allan Disappears

We decided that we shouldn't disturb the old stone slab we had found. Mr. Allan had said not to touch it until we went over with him, so we just fooled around all day waiting for him to come back. We played ball for a while, and then we went over and looked at Terry's canoe. We said he should put another coat of paint on it, that the canvas still showed. Terry said that was the way he liked it. He was going to sand it down some more and put another coat on, but that when he was through the canvas would still show. Terry really does a good job when he paints a canoe.

The next morning we were at school bright and early. Every child in the settlement was there, for Mr. Allan taught us all. We were in two rooms. One of the older boys or girls would keep order in each room while Mr. Allan walked from one room to the other teaching the classes.

Some people say that all we ever learn, we learn from one or two teachers ... if we are lucky enough to meet a real teacher. Mr. Allan was a real teacher. Besides our regular lessons, he read to us from other books. He read poetry to us too, and we began to like it. He told us stories of the history of the past, Rome and Greece, China, England, and how the Magna Carta led to the American Revolution. On days when we had done our lessons well, he would sometimes bring out the globe and point to some of the places he had been. He had traveled a lot.

Well, that day we sat around the

schoolhouse, and we sat around there, and about an hour and a half after school was supposed to start, Mr. Allan hadn't shown up.

Nan suddenly ran out of the door calling, "I'm going down and tell my mother there is no school today!"

We said, "Come back here! There is going to be school. Mr. Allan will be here." But after another hour he still had not come.

Well, you know how it is. Everyone started throwing things and carrying on, so we decided to wander down to the beach for a swim.

We walked along the beach to the Outer Island slough. Before we went in the water we rested on the sand for a while. I watched the steady flight of some pelicans. Way out we could see some porpoises jumping.

Bill was a great swimmer, but Terry could stay under water longer than any of us. Roy could run. Roy and I took a sudden spurt, scattering the sandpipers. He won, but only by a little bit. His red hair was standing on end. His freckled face wore a triumphant grin.

"You get the prize." Terry picked up a conch shell and handed it to Roy.

"That's a beauty," I said. "I wish I'd found it." I held it to my ear to hear the roar of the sea.

"Do you want it? Take it," said Roy. "Saves me the trouble of toting it."

Bill was first in the water. He moved like a porpoise without disturbing the surface. His dark hair caught the light where the sun had faded it. He was the last out of the water.

We were already shaking out our clothes. We always do that before we put them back on, and it's a good habit. When Roy shook out his trousers that day, a rattlesnake tumbled out. Bill grabbed a long stick and killed it. The snake had crawled in the clothes to get out of the sun.

As we passed my house I left the conch shell on the porch. My mother was making a border of conches around a flower bed of verbena and zinnias. I knew she would be pleased.

We went by Mr. Parker's store. We were killing time there when somebody came along and asked what we were doing out of school. We answered that Mr. Allan hadn't come.

Mr. Parker said, "Go down and see if he's sick." So we went on down to his house, but it was still locked up the way it had been the day before. There was no sign of him, and his boat was still missing.

Back in town when we told them at the post office that he had gone, we didn't know where, the whole place began to be stirred up. Where was Mr. Allan?

"Yesterday was a calm day. There was no reason for his not returning in his boat." Mr. Parker is considered the unofficial commissioner of the community. There's no law on our island. So after a while, he and Mr. Toomey and Mr. Baker said they had better go and see where Mr. Allan was. They were all on the school committee.

A bunch of us followed them to Mr. Allan's house. Of course they looked all around, and they tried to see through the shutters. At last they decided that he had really gone. They turned around and said, "But where? And why today? Monday is a school day."

We all walked back together. Where was Mr. Allan? Everyone was asking, "Have you seen Mr. Allan?" "Have you seen Mr. Allan?" But no one had.

Mr. Parker announced that there would still be school. "You children get on back to the schoolhouse." So he sent his grown daughter to teach us. She used to teach us every once in a while before Mr. Allan came. We all wandered back to school, but she let us out in about an hour. She couldn't keep order that day.

We were really worried. Finally, we decided that since we were out early we would take the rowboat across to Center Island. We jumped into the boat and took turns at the oars. It's quite a piece over there. The other day, rowing across to see Mr. Allan, it had seemed awfully short. We had really crossed in a hurry, but now we weren't talking as much and it seemed twice as long.

As soon as we landed, we climbed to the ridge on a trot. I don't know why we were so anxious to get there. Perhaps the same thought was in all our minds.

We saw at once that someone had been there, for there was the big old coquina slab pulled back. Not all the way, just partly, so that you could look down into the shallow vault. It was empty. We took a stick and poked around in it to be sure. Bill tore off a piece of his shirttail and threw it into the vault to reflect the sun. We couldn't figure out how we could move that top slab a little more so that we could see better. We used some saplings and a pole and pried at it. It moved a little bit at a time, a little bit at a time, so that we could squeeze our heads down in there and really see. It was completely empty, but it looked as though a chest or something of that shape had been resting in there. We could see the marks. We looked at each other, and all said at once, "What do you think of that?" We meant the same thing . . . Mr. Allan had been there before us!

We took a good look inside but it told us nothing more, only that something had been in there. We worked until nearly dark getting the slab back and covering the vault. Then we threw sand on it and covered it with branches

and brushed out our tracks. We knew we had better go home.

As we went down through the twilight, a gray heron lifted itself into the air and flew ahead of us, its great wings flapping slowly. I guess it was going home too.

We rowed as hard as we could, but we all caught the dickens for being late that night.

Next day we were at school early. Mr. Allan didn't come. In both rooms they were saying, "I wonder what happened to Mr. Allan?" We just looked at each other. *We* wondered what had happened to Mr. Allan!

All over East Edge all you heard was, "Where's Mr. Allan?" "What happened to Mr. Allan?" Every time a boat came back to port, everybody wanted to know, had they heard anything of Mr. Allan or his boat?

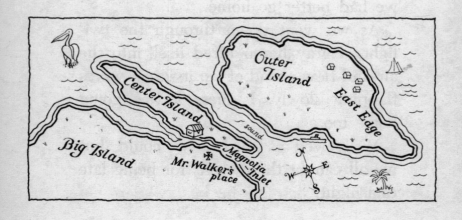

The Captain from the White Ship Asks an Astonishing Question

A few days later a big white yacht —
more than a yacht really, a small ship —
came into the sound and tied up at the
shrimp docks. We went down to see it.
It was a great sight. It had all kinds of
gear. One place where a door was open
we could see a cabin . . . polished wood
and brass, and curtains at the portholes.
It was no fishing boat!

The four of us inspected that ship.
She smelled of paint and tar and wet
rope, and all mingled with the salt in the
air. They were flying a foreign flag that
nobody recognized. We could see a
diving suit hanging up in the cabin. On

the deck was a compressor and equipment of various kinds. Everyone in East Edge strolled by to take a look. We hadn't had a visitor like this ship in all our combined lives. Some handsome vessels had come in, but this was a sea-going scout. It no sooner tied up than the nicest looking varnished sea skiff you ever saw was slung over the side into the water. The Captain came ashore and asked, "Where will I find the mayor?"

Bill said, "You mean Commissioner Parker, don't you?"

"Is he in charge?"

One of us answered, "Yes, he's in charge."

Roy explained, "He's the postmaster."

"Where will I find him?"

"Most likely at the post office."

"Where is the post office?" He sounded a bit impatient. He was a tall, wind-bitten man, strong and dark, but in spite of that foreign flag you couldn't be sure what he was: not an American anyhow. He had just a trace of an accent — kind of British, like Mr. Allan.

"Why, the post office is up in the store. Mr. Parker's store."

So the Captain, who sounded awfully English for a foreigner, made a sign to the Mate — I guess it was the Mate — and started off to Mr. Parker's store. The Mate had been staring at the four of us, as though he would like to boil us in oil.

He had wicked eyes. He was a bearded man with a bush of hair. I noticed as he followed the Captain that, even with his back turned, he was a frightening man.

We followed them.

Mr. Parker had come out on that little porch he had on the front of his store. He was tall and rather thin. He was young, but his light brown hair had a little gray at the temples. He was a kind man; his eyes always seemed to smile when he looked at you. He spoke gently, but his word was law. He was out on his porch when the Captain walked up with the Mate, and they said, "Howdy," and the Captain asked Mr. Parker if he was in charge of the place. Mr. Parker said, "Not exactly, I'm the postmaster."

So guess what the Captain asked — "Where will I find Mr. Allan?" Boy, did that stop us in our tracks!

Mr. Parker said, "Who?" as though he had never heard of Mr. Allan. We didn't know why he did that. Then Mr. Parker said, "What do you want with this Mr. Allan? Who is he?"

All the East Edge people who happened to be hanging around picked up the cue from Mr. Parker, and they said they didn't know who Mr. Allan was either. All of a sudden we caught on too. We weren't supposed to know Mr. Allan.

The Captain went into the store, and we tried to follow them, but Mr. Parker said, "Not now, boys!" and we knew we had better wait outside.

After a while the Captain came out smoking a cigar that Mr. Parker had given him. I think Mr. Parker figured on selling him a lot of supplies. The Mate had a cigar too. As they were leaving they both spoke to Mr. Parker and we noticed that the Mate spoke English with an accent quite different from the Captain's accent. We never did figure it out.

The four of us tagged along behind them to the docks. We were puzzled. What was it all about? We didn't even have any questions to ask each other. But why hadn't Mr. Parker said that Mr. Allan had disappeared? Why didn't he say that he knew him, that he was an awfully nice man? Mr. Parker liked Mr. Allan.

Bill said, "Mr. Parker thinks those men are the law. They are looking for Mr. Allan, and Mr. Parker thinks that Mr. Allan must have gone away for a good reason. That's about what it was."

Things began to happen. I don't know how they found out where Mr. Allan's house was, but the next day there were a couple of sailors and the Mate with the Captain wandering around there. They went up and down Mill Creek in their skiff and flashed over the sound, foam in their wake. Once or twice they landed on Center Island. We saw them in the distance walking along the shore. They were certainly looking for something. No doubt Mr. Allan!

School had come to a standstill. Mr. Parker's daughter had to go to Santa Maria to see an aunt who was sick. Everyone in East Edge was talking about what we would do for a teacher, or even for someone to keep us in the school-house all morning.

The four of us went camping. Terry's canoe certainly did come in handy. We used it all the time now instead of the rowboat. We could get around fast in that canoe. Our parents often let us spend a night on one of the islands, and we made camp on the ridge on Center Island. For one thing, we could see East Edge and the docks from there, and we could keep our eyes on the ship.

A funny thing — except for the two sailors who were sometimes with the Mate or the Captain — the crew from the foreign ship were always busy. They did not speak to anyone in East Edge. They were never seen fishing, or anything like that. They were always working on their gear, or on deck, or painting the sides of the ship. Yes, they were very busy. Sometimes several of them would go off together in the sea skiff. We watched them running up and down the ladders, going some place.

On Saturday they had a big bundle of mail, most of it addressed to Captain Da Costa. We were at Mr. Parker's store when the weekly mail sack came in.

After dinner that day I overheard my father tell my mother that Mr. Parker had had a note from Mr. Allan. It was mailed from Santa Maria the day after he left. My father said Mr. Parker didn't want the news to get around. All the note said was, "Called away. Return indefinite. Please give my salary to a substitute teacher."

I had been eavesdropping, so I thought the less said by me the better. It didn't change anything anyhow.

By this time we had fixed up quite a camp for ourselves on Center Island. We cleaned out the brush and hauled over a big tarpaulin, two shovels, and other things. We made the camp a little way back from the top, where no one could see it.

Trapped
on the White Ship

We had watched the white ship, named *Venator de Gaza,* many times after it tied up at the main dock. Everyone in East Edge idled by whenever possible to give it a good going over with the eye. We had sort of hung around in that vicinity ever since the ship had docked. By now we knew pretty well the routine of the sailors. We had watched them all day, from early in the morning until after the sun went down.

One evening at twilight we had been lying on the flat roof of a shed that was near the ship when we decided to go aboard. We saw that the sailor on watch had gone astern to listen to one of the fellows playing a guitar in a shrimp boat tied up behind the white ship. It was growing darker by the minute; we could just barely see him leaning over the rail.

The gangplank was well forward and it was in shadow. We had made up our minds to board. So we crawled over the gangplank in a bunch, hoping not to be seen, and, I guess, to protect each other. We crawled along, our noses about an inch above the deck. There was a sweet, clean smell from the planking, like a freshly scrubbed kitchen floor. We continued to nose our way toward the black darkness of the forward wall of the main cabin. Light was streaming from two high port openings.

None of us had made a sound. Terry motioned to me to stand up so that he could get on my shoulders. With Bill holding him, he told us in a whisper what he saw through the porthole.

It was a large cabin. He could see

four men, and the legs of a fifth man who was seated just below the porthole. Two of the men were standing in front of large maps on the opposite wall and pointing out something on them. One man was the Captain, and the other the man who had been with him the day they talked to Mr. Parker at the post office. The other two men he could see were on opposite sides of a table cleaning guns. All wore the ship's uniform.

Then Terry whispered that he could see the maps as the men moved around. They were big maps, one for each of the islands: Outer Island, Center Island, and Big Island. Terry's eyes were gleaming, and his voice sounded hoarse.

Then Roy wanted to get in the act. He had to see for himself. There was a tall, narrow barrel lashed upright to the bulkhead of a forward hatch, and Roy managed to climb onto it some way, to try to see into the other port opening. As he leaned forward to look, a wooden lid that was covering the top of the barrel flipped, and Roy went into the barrel with a grunt. Bill somehow caught the wooden top before it hit the deck. Terry was off my shoulders in a flash, and the three of us were at the barrel in a second. It was bad. Roy was scared. He thought at first he had fallen into some kind of a trap. It might as well have been a trap, for it amounted to the same thing. The barrel contained a sounding line that had been carefully coiled, and it happened that Roy's feet went in together in a perfect feet-first dive. The line had slipped down around him, as though someone were wrapping up the lower half of a mummy. He couldn't move. His legs were held by the rope. When he tried to move them, it felt as though the rope squeezed tighter.

Terry had the idea of feeding the line out on deck, "but then it could be 100 fathoms long," he added. Yet it seemed the only thing to do. We were trying to figure out how to feed out the line and at the same time to unwrap it from around Roy, when suddenly things became very, very quiet. The music from the guitar had stopped. Only the blowers sounding faintly in the open stack near us gave a sense of life to the ship. But it was like the breath of an animal crouching for attack.

Bill slipped quickly to the edge of the cabin and peered around toward the stern to check on the sailor. "He's starting to come up this way," he said in a low voice. "Now he's stopped to light his pipe. We'd better get off while we can!"

Terry said to Roy in the barrel, "We'll be back, but we must try to get off now. Someone is coming. I'll put the cover on, but put the end of the rope over the edge so you can get some air in from the crack. Be quiet. We'll knock three times when we get back."

"Be as quick as you can," said Roy.

"You bet," I said.

The only way to get off was the way we had come. We crawled back to the gangplank and down it in scrambling haste, keeping together as well as we could. When we reached the foot of the gangplank, still stooping together, we heard a loud "ahoy!" from the ship.

"Ahoy," the sailor repeated, "what are you doing there?"

Terry answered. "One of us lost something."

Bill added quickly, "Here it is! We've found it!" Then he said under his breath, "Follow me," and ran down the dock toward the village. Terry and I were not far behind, and the three of us raced over the wharf.

As soon as we were sure that the sailor was not following, we stopped. We leaned against some pilings, so we couldn't be seen in the darkness, and had a confab. We tried to figure out how we could get Roy loose in a hurry. It would take time to unwrap him. The line might be snarled. We had to be ready for anything. Getting back on board wasn't going to be easy either. Then we reasoned that if we boarded safely, we should bring Roy some food. Then if it took a long time to free him, he wouldn't be too hungry, even if we had to leave him again.

First things first. We headed for my house, as it was the nearest, to see what we could find in the way of food. We passed the fresh-water pump on our way and Bill suggested that we wash our hands before going into my mother's kitchen. Terry thought we should bring a bottle back with us to take some water to Roy.

My house was dark. We went in the back way. I struck a match and found the lamp.

The warming oven had a pan of delicious looking brown fried fish. It was still hot and it had that great smell that makes your mouth water. While I picked out some nice boneless pieces, Terry took a freshly baked loaf of bread from the screened safe. He began cutting slices for all of us. The odor of that good food filled the kitchen. We moved very quickly. I told Bill where to find an empty bottle in the pantry. Terry put back what was left of the loaf. I wrapped up a sandwich for Roy, and put a piece of fish on a slice of bread for each of us.

"Let's get going," I said.

"Will your mother be mad?" asked Bill.

"No, but I'll leave a note," I answered, and I scribbled on a piece of paper our thanks for the fish.

We began to eat as soon as we were on our way back to the ship. We hadn't wasted a moment. As soon as we finished eating, we changed our pace from a trot to a sprint.

We didn't know how we were going to get aboard. We wanted to be as near to the ship as possible, so that we could sneak on the first chance we had.

We were worried about Roy. He was stuck in such a position that we didn't see how he could move even a little bit. It was tougher than we guessed, as we found out from Roy later.

"What if we can't get on?" asked Terry.

"We *have* to!" Bill and I answered together.

One shed on the dock had a great advantage for us, and that's where we headed. There was a pile of waterfront gear around it, bait boxes, crayfish traps, an upturned dory, a few oil drums and the like that gave good cover, and it was easy to climb up on the roof without being seen from the ship. From there we could see the deck and the man on watch. Also, it was near the gangplank. We hugged the edge of the dock, although it was a moonless night. We had noticed that the sailor on watch usually sat on a canvas stool amidships so as to get a good view straight down the dock toward land.

When we reached the shed no time was lost. We decided that we would try to board the ship one at a time. Bill would go first and take the food and water for Roy. I had wrapped a sandwich in oil paper for Roy, and Bill managed to get it into his pocket. It had dawned on us that Roy had not had anything to eat since noon.

Now we had to think of some way to distract the sailor on watch. There he was, standing up at the rail and wide awake! We couldn't think of anything short of pretending to drown. But that sort of thing has a way of backfiring, so we never really considered it.

Fate came to the rescue. A couple of shrimpers on the way back to their boat from the village were having a loud argument. One said that it didn't matter if they missed the turning of the tide when they sailed, and the other said that the exact timing of the tide was as important as death and birth. As they passed alongside the white ship, the sailor on watch walked astern to keep pace with them and listen to what they were saying. They were loud, and each repeated the same argument over and over.

Bill took off, his body bent over, a swift dark shadow moving over to the gangplank, then up on it, onto the deck. He disappeared into the darkness under the lights forward from the main cabin.

Over the shouting of the shrimpers, we could hear the sailor telling them to be quiet. "I tell you the answer," he called. "The tide is important. The one that says the timing of the tide must not be missed is right. Listen to me!"

We thought the noise would bring out some of the others on the ship. Now or never. I took off up the gangplank, crawling fast.

When I reached the barrel, Roy was wolfing down the fish and bread, and saying between bites to tell Larry to tell his mother that it was the greatest fish he had ever tasted, and did he need it.

Then he told us how two of the sailors, or perhaps they were officers — he hadn't dared to look out — had stood there smoking and talking. They spoke of the wonderful meal they had just eaten: fried shrimp, boiled shrimp, plates of crabmeat, and a marvelous fish that might have been flounder, and they praised the vegetables too. Roy said he thought at first that they knew he was in the barrel, and that he was hungry, and that they were having fun with him. Then one said they would be leaving all this good sea food soon. The other asked if he knew when. The first man answered that the skipper had said any time now. As soon as they finished with that fellow Allan, they would put to sea at once.

"They said that?" asked Bill, astonished. He offered the bottle of water to Roy. "Do you suppose that means they know where he is?"

Roy didn't answer. He said, "Get that water out of the barrel! Do you want me to be squeezed to death? That's the way the Indians did it . . . tie a victim up and wet the rope around him, so that it keeps tightening up. I'm already being squeezed to a pulp! I'm sweating. How about getting me out of here?"

Terry had come by then and said he would stand at the corner of the cabin and keep an eye on the sailor.

We decided to feed the line out of the barrel and over the side of the ship away from the dock. Then when Roy was out of the barrel we would slide down that way into the water and swim ashore. The tide was coming in pretty strong about then, and that would help

us clear the ship fast and come to shore
a good distance away.

The night was awfully dark. Bill suggested that we cut a good length of the
rope so that we could keep together by

holding on to it after we were in the water. He borrowed Terry's knife and we started unwrapping Roy. It was as though we were unwrapping a ball of twine, tight in a water glass. Bill said maybe we could cut the coil of rope from around Roy.

Roy said nothing doing. There was so much line in the barrel that he would never get loose, and we could be cutting the same turn of the line several times . . . everything was too tight.

Bill was up on the hatch bulkhead lifting the rope around Roy's shoulders and head with every turn of the line, and I began feeding it over the rail.

There was a hissing sound from Terry. "Skipper!" he whispered. Bill dropped the rope and joined Terry. I followed. We could see the skipper in a doorway down near the stern. There was a faint red light from a lantern down that way. The sailor was just a pale blur. The skipper spoke in a loud voice that we could hear only too clearly.

"What's going on up here? Did I hear shouting and running on the deck?"

"Oh, no," the sailor said. "There was no running." He explained that he was trying to quiet a couple of loudmouths who were passing on the dock.

"Well," said the Captain, "carry on, then." We could hear the heavy door slam as he left the deck.

That was close. My hands were cold. Without a word we went back to the barrel and tried to speed things up. Terry kept coming back to ask how we were doing. The sailor was pacing back and forth in the middle of the ship.

Roy tried to help by holding up the rope each time it unwound, but he had a hard time keeping his hands and arms out of the way.

At first I let the line down over the top of the rail. Then I thought better of it and took a tuck in it and put it over the side under the bottom rail. Now if anyone started walking on deck it wouldn't hit them in the chest. But there was a slight noise as the line came back and dropped underneath, pulled by the weight of the line Bill was handing me. The little sound made me nervous. I wondered how far it would carry on such a still night. At last Bill gave a quick double jerk on the rope, and I went to the barrel. Roy said he thought he was free enough from the coil of rope now, but he couldn't move. He felt paralyzed.

I touched Terry on the shoulder and beckoned, and the three of us somehow lifted Roy out of the barrel. Roy's arms were strong, and he put one around Bill's neck and one around mine. For a minute it was like a death grip. Terry swung Roy's legs out of the barrel and Roy was free, but now he couldn't stand. We sat him down with his back against the wall. Terry went back to his watch at the corner, and Bill and I began rubbing Roy's legs.

"Stop," he said. "Wait a minute. I can't take it. It feels funny." He spoke in a very low voice, but any sound seemed risky now.

Now our problem was getting off the ship. It would be impossible to go down the gangplank carrying Roy; yet even if we should get him over the rail and into the water, could he keep afloat?

Terry came up to us. "Get him on his feet," he urged. "It looks as though the sailor is coming this way." He went back.

We put our arms under Roy's arms and lifted him. He said he could feel his legs. There was a sharp tingling. Very unpleasant. "I guess they went to sleep," he said. "I thought I was paralyzed." It was a minute or two before Roy decided that he would walk again. When he could stand by himself we felt better.

"Step on it!" Terry said rushing to join

us. "He's coming." Then he said, "Go on, I'll follow you." He went back to look at the sailor.

Bill made the line fast to the railing. It was the quickest thing I ever saw. Then he went down the line, and I helped Roy over. Terry was beside me, lending a hand. "It's O.K.," he said. "Another sailor just came out, and they are talking."

I went over and Terry came after me. Bill and I swam close to Roy, so that if he had a cramp we could pound it out. We all held on to the cut piece of rope and kept close together. We did not try to swim until we had drifted quite a way from the ship on the tide. Then we swam hard for shore.

A Yellow Face

I remember the campfire the next night, and the supper we prepared, because it was then that Terry had his great idea. His few words changed the whole picture, and led us to half of a puzzle. Before that puzzle was solved it would uncover forgotten history, and threaten at least one life.

It had been a fine meal. Corn on the cob, roasted potatoes, some of the best brim I've ever tasted. No, it was sea trout, the brim was another time. I mustn't get ahead of my story. We buried the corn in the coals with the shucks on. We would wet them, peel them back, take the silks out, then tie the shucks around, dip them in salt water, and put them in the embers. Awfully good. We cooked the potatoes in the wood coals too.

We were sitting around not saying a word, looking into the driftwood fire we had built in the scooped-out sand. Every once in a while it would give off a green flame or a blue flame because the wood had been soaked in the salts of the sea. Beyond the fire the stars were beginning to come out.

Suddenly Terry said, "You know, we've forgotten something."

We said, "You can say that again!" But we didn't know what he meant.

"I'm not kidding. You know what Mr. Allan said: 'When you find something, keep digging down, keep digging. There might be something below that find. In the early days, Indians kept coming back to the same campsite. Be careful. Keep digging deeper.' "

We remembered Mr. Allan's saying that.

"Well, we didn't dig deeper," said Terry. His eyes, which were big anyway, looked bigger and darker in the firelight.

We sat up too, thinking about what he had said. No, we had not even examined the site very thoroughly. We could hardly sleep that night.

At daybreak next morning we were up and digging around the vault. We heaped up brush beside it to hide it from the path. One of us was on the lookout all the time to be sure that no one could come up and surprise us. We kept digging along the sides of the slabs forming the vault, and then all of a sudden we let out a whoop! We had hit another stone underneath, protruding a little from the top one. It was the same construction as the vault above. Roy was on watch on the ridge and he came running. We dug on just one side now and made sure of what we had found. There was certainly another boxlike shape under the first one.

Now, how would we get the top one off the bottom one, when we could hardly move the top slab? We'd have to go and bring a block and tackle, but how would we rig it up? We'd have to make an 'A' frame or something like that, to hold . it up . . . to hoist it out. We didn't know too much about how to do it, but we had seen them work on boats and engines around the docks.

We talked as though we knew what we were talking about. We cleaned around the four sides and saw more clearly that we had really hit something, we didn't know what. There was another vault under the first one. How could we get into it?

For two days we couldn't think of a way to move those stones.

In East Edge we tried to get hold of a block and tackle, but we couldn't find anyone on the wharf who would lend it to us. They wanted to know what we were going to use it for. We didn't tell them, so we were left on our own.

Each of us had chores to do at home, but we resented every minute we could not spend on the island.

Something was nearly in our hands, and we just circled around it helplessly.

On the third day we decided that the only way to do it was to skid the whole thing off, the way we did the slab. Only it would be bigger and harder. We must get the top slab off again to lessen the weight. So we cut some small logs. They were kind of green and slippery. In half an afternoon of work we pushed off the top slab and left it resting on the logs. Then we dug the slanted ledge the other way and put logs there, still with the bark on, just below the bottom of the vault.

It took more than two days, working hours each day to push that stone box off. We would cover up what we had done with old dead brush and go away, and then the next chance we had, we'd be back digging and chopping, pushing and pulling. The empty vault was scooped out of coquina, tied together with metal bands on the corners. They were big stones like the ones held down by iron clamps and used for sidewalks in old St. Augustine. The vault finally skidded off in a rush.

Just as we moved it off and could see the top of the box beneath, the Mate from the white ship and one of the sailors came in sight just below the ridge. They had walked along the marsh so we hadn't seen them land.

We grabbed the tarpaulin. We grabbed the pole and stuck it up in the middle. Bill stood there on the lid of the vault and held the pole in the hole. We pulled out the corners of the tarpaulin as if it were a tent. It just covered our digging and the stones.

Three of us moved out on the path as the men were coming up and stood in their way.

The Mate said something to the sailor with him. It sounded like, "This is where the smoke was coming from." Then he wanted to know how long we had been camping there. We said we always camped there. It was our camping place. They seemed most curious about the tarpaulin and the way it was rigged up. Why did we let it droop down that way? Terry said it made it cooler in the daytime when the sun was hot. So they let it go at that. Bill was still under the tarpaulin sweating it out. The pole shook a few times. They didn't notice, but we did. Finally they went down back to the water.

As soon as they had gone, Bill came out of the hole. He crawled out and began slapping his left leg and limping about. It seems that while he was steadying the pole under the tarpaulin, his leg had been wedged against the side, and it went to sleep. He had felt it tingling, and at the same time felt two or three small fiddler crabs running over his feet. He could wriggle his right foot but he didn't dare move much. The pole and the tarp were so unsteady, he was afraid they might fall over. He had kept the little fiddlers off his right foot, but the other foot was powerless. He could only hope that they wouldn't gnaw him. Now he was a funny sight, hopping and slapping and limping and looking at his leg as he hobbled about to see if the fiddler crabs had chewed him up. We began to laugh. The more we laughed, the madder he grew, and the angrier he was, the more we laughed. We couldn't help it.

"Where did those fiddlers come from in that hole all of a sudden?" he demanded. His gray eyes, usually so quiet, looked black.

We laughed again until we rolled on the ground. "Did you think we let them loose in there just to bother you?" asked Roy.

Bill said he still had no feeling in his leg.

"How about a drink of water?" I asked.

"I could use it," said Bill in a calmer tone. I poured a cupful for him. Then he laughed too.

"We had better get back to work," Terry said.

The lid we were trying to slide off was not quite as heavy as the first one, and we managed, all pushing together, to put small logs under the front end. There were words in a strange language carved on this lid also, mysterious to us, but they seemed the same as on the first one. Perhaps the skids were firmer, or we had somehow caught the knack of it, but anyway suddenly off it came, sliding to the third side of the hole.

Inside was a chest. Were we excited! A dark and ancient chest. It didn't fill

the bottom of the vault, so in our eager-
ness two of us reached down to try to
open it, to see what was in it. We saw
in a moment that we would have to take
the chest out of the vault before it could
be opened. We used the rope we had,
tying it onto the metal handles on the
ends. Using saplings and making a ful-
crum, we lifted it out. When we took up
on the lines it came up easily. It was not
very heavy. There were thin metal
bands on the top about every five inches.

The top was sloping. Then we saw that it didn't have a lock. We examined it and found that there were long bolts, but we couldn't figure out how to slide them back. Finally we found an end piece which swung down so that the bolts could slide out. It was interesting the way it was locked. We flung the lid back.

We didn't know what to expect. There was a jumble of oilskins. We lifted them out and saw that they covered a number of what appeared to be long tubes wrapped carefully in oilskins. We opened two of them and saw .that they were rolled-up maps. These maps seemed to be all that the chest had in it. We unrolled the maps one by one.

"This is drawn on a kind of thin leather," said Bill.

We crowded in to look. I felt it. "I believe it's that vellum he told us about," I said. I was pleased that I had remembered the word.

"That's just what it is," said Roy.

We held the map between us, so that we could all examine it. It was only half a map. We looked at another, and then another. They were all drawn on the same stuff. Each one was only half a map. And not one map fitted any other! They seemed to have been deliberately torn. Perhaps the missing portions had been destroyed. They were maps of our islands all right. Even with the foreign names on them, we could tell that much.

"Look at this one," said Terry. "This is the sound. Don't you think it's the shape of Outer Island, this part of it. This is the harbor by the look of it, but it's torn right across."

"Maybe this is the only part of it they wanted to keep," I suggested.

"We must study them and see why they only kept these pieces. Could this be the old fort?" Roy put his freckled face close to the carefully drawn spot in red and dark blue.

"It could be. I can't get my bearings. One thing is sure, they are not much good as they are." Bill rolled up the map he was holding and wrapped it in the oilskin. We rolled them all up and put them back into the chest. I pulled the loose oilskins over them and tucked them in. My hand struck something hard and stiff in the bottom of the chest.

"Here's something else . . . a square thing," I said. I lifted out the flat package. They all came close. I unwrapped it cautiously and handed the oilskin to Bill. It was a foot square, a little longer perhaps than wide. The first thing we saw, lying loosely on the top of it, was a layer of wax, about as thick as that on a homemade jar of preserves. We took it off.

Underneath was a painting. Even to our eyes it was a very good painting. It was the head of a man with a yellow face, very handsome, young, with wavy hair. Somehow we knew it was from long ago. It was a brave face, but *all* was a dark yellow . . . not only the face, but the hair, the whole head. There was a strange look about the eyes, and the head was not on a body but was resting on a table. We were awed. There was something outside of ordinary life in the face of this man. In the background of the painting was a beautiful landscape in soft blues and greens, but very small, seen through a window high up, and the center of the scene was a boy riding a wild white horse.

We each examined the painting. Bill turned it over. It was painted on a board. The wood was very old. A name was written or painted on the back in rather small letters. It looked like U Tucci. And beneath it was stamped or drawn the same coat of arms that had been carved on the slab of the vault. Right away we knew that we had something rare.

"Look at the eyes," said Terry. "That almost blind look."

I took it into my hands with respect and looked again at the puzzling face. "Fellows," I said, "that is not meant to be a portrait. I think it is the painting of a part of a statue."

A Voice
in the Storm

The camp near the ridge was far too open. We decided that we should hide the chest somewhere else.

In order to haul the chest, we would have to make a sled of some sort and slide it along. We lashed together a sled that looked pretty good. We made the lines tight and left two long ones to pull it with.

All this time one of us was on the lookout to be sure that no one was coming up the ridge or prowling about.

North on Center Island we had another campsite where we could swim. It was on the side of a bluff, and we had a small cave there. We had been there many times. In the cave we had a large oil drum which we had half buried in the earth to use as a table. Now Terry suggested that we dig up the drum and use it to hide the chest in. There was a deep spot in the cave hard to get into. We figured that if we could push the drum back there and bank it with sand, it would be a fine hiding place.

Before we started off for the cave we had a lot of work to do. We would have liked to move the slabs back to the way we had found them, but that was impossible, so we gathered brush and filled in the hole. We used the logs and saplings we had to cover up. We did a good job. We also put some bramble bushes around the spot. We planned to do it right later.

We couldn't take all our gear along with the chest, so we decided that we would come back and camp near the vault. (A poor decision as it turned

out.) We wrapped the chest with the tarpaulin, and put our gear under some trees where it would be sheltered. Then we pulled the chest over the slope of the ridge toward the marsh. One of us walked behind the sled, to hold it back with a line as we went down the slope. He also brushed off the marks behind us with a branch of twigs he was carrying. We changed places quite often, pulling and holding back.

When we were finally down, we rigged up the lines so that we could pull the sled single file to make a narrow track through the marsh, and off we went. It slipped well enough over the long grass of the wet land, and it didn't take long to get to the cave.

We dug up the drum. That wasn't hard. We saw that the chest would go in with plenty of clearance. First we pushed the drum into the back and dug a place for it in the wall. Then we put the chest in and heaped the sand. Of course we hadn't rested. The sight of the chest had changed us all. We hadn't let up since we saw it. We all felt curiously important.

After we had buried the chest we had to clean up and remove any signs of what we had done. It seemed as if we had been digging forever. It was almost morning when we finished. We were beginning to know that we were exhausted, but we thought we had better haul the sled as far from the cave as possible. Again we were careful to brush out all tracks as we went back into the marsh.

Going back was easy. We took turns, one of us riding while the other three pulled. Morning broke as we set out, but there were dark clouds and it looked like stormy weather setting in. We agreed that we had better gather up our gear and head back to East Edge and home.

It was comfortable riding on the sled covered with a tarpaulin. We didn't mind the brief spells of rain — just sudden flurries that didn't last long. The wind was rising, and soon the rain began to come down hard and cold. We knew we were really in for a storm.

We were nearly at the campsite. We took the sled apart and scattered the logs along the water's edge. We hoped it would look as though we used them for landing a boat. We carried ropes and tarpaulin together. We were so tired we could hardly climb to the ridge.

Terry reached the top first. We heard an agonized shout. "The canoe!" He pointed to the open water where the canoe was bobbing up and down in the angry turbulent waters of the sound. We had pulled it carefully up beyond the tide's line, but the wind had blown it away.

The wind hit us too. We braced ourselves as we looked toward East Edge. The clouds made a sullen gray tent overhead. Whitecapped waves were rushing all over the sound. The white ship had gone. There was only one shrimp boat left. We could see people running and climbing aboard. Gusts of wind were really coming, forty or fifty miles an hour. There on the ridge we could hardly stand up against it. We decided that we had better batten down below the ridge somewhere.

Without the canoe we had no way to get home. We had to find a hiding place from the storm.

We found some sand dunes on the lee side, where we were protected from the worst of it. Of course we had some wind. When we started a fire the wind and the rain put it out. The rain was coming down so hard that we could not rig up the tarpaulin. We were soaked, so we just huddled under it, the rain pelting, the wind rising. We were in for a storm all right, but we couldn't figure out where to go. We couldn't possibly make it back to the cave, as the wind would be driving against us.

All of a sudden we heard a voice coming from the palmettos and pines just beyond where we were, to the south of us.

"Hi, fellows!" it called.

Of course I was sure it was the wind,

but the others seemed to have heard it too. Roy laughed a little and said, "The wind making a sound like that!"

Then we heard, "Don't be nervous now, fellows. I'm coming to see you!" And to our amazement, on a gust of wind, came a tall man with a beard.

We didn't recognize him until he was right on top of us. His blue eyes seemed even bluer, his face and arms browned by the weather. It was Mr. Allan! His trousers were torn off up to the knees. His shirt was torn. He was kind of wild looking, but he talked as if we had just left him a few minutes ago at his house.

"You had better get your gear together," he said. "We'll try to make my camp. There's a shack there, and I have some food. We should walk on the west side and head south. I am quite far south, almost at the end of the island. There's worse weather coming. It may be a hurricane."

We didn't know what to think. None of us had said more than "Hi!" to him. We were remembering that Mr. Allan had walked out on us, but he calmly took charge. As he talked, he was helping us get our tools together, packing up, rolling up the tarpaulin. It was a heavy tarpaulin. It took two of us boys to carry it. But Mr. Allan slung it across one shoulder. We scrambled the rest of the gear together, picked up the shovels, and followed him. There was all that wind and rain beating on us, and we knew that worse was brewing.

Mr. Allan said, "I tried to make it to

East Edge when I saw what the sky looked like. I thought I might be needed there, but I didn't get far. My boat turned over and I had to swim back. It was tough trying to reach shore. I landed just below here. I could hardly believe my eyes when I saw a little smoke coming from the other side of the ridge. Then it disappeared, but I climbed up and found you here."

"We came to camp and we didn't notice how bad the weather was until we saw our canoe floating away," said Bill.

We went down the ridge and started to push through the marsh on the west side. The wind was really whipping. When it hit us in the face it nearly took the skin off. Branches, too, slashed at us.

Mr. Allan said, "It hasn't started blowing yet, but it's really going to blow!"

The trees in the distance were bent nearly double, and there was a terrible whistling sound in the air. The waters were stirred up even in the marsh. We could hear a roaring in the distance as though the sea would overwhelm us. I didn't see how it could be any worse.

Mr. Allan stopped short. "We'll never never make it to my camp," he said. "We'll try for the bluff. It's not far." He said there was good protection where the bluff was. In bygone days people used to keep their boats there. There used to be a boat landing too.

We were bent over against the wind. It seemed as though Mr. Allan was carrying everything. He had the shovels, his arms were full of gear, and the tarpaulin was over his shoulder. He took something from each of us as we walked through the marsh. He led the way, walking faster than we could keep up. His shoes seemed about worn out, but it didn't seem to bother him. He went through even the saw grass as if it were nothing at all.

We knew that cove, but we never used it for a camp. We went under the bluff a little way. There was a spot there with protection on two sides, from the east and from the south. There was an overhang too, which helped a lot.

Mr. Allan suggested that we dig back a little to make a kind of cave to help shelter us. We did what we could in a few minutes of frantic shoveling. We put our gear back underneath the bluff, spread out the tarpaulin, and then, as though on signal, the rain started pouring. I had thought it was raining before. This was a flood from the skies.

The one thing we had left behind on the ridge was most of our grub. Terry had picked up a canvas bag that had potatoes in it. That was all.

The rain pounded, and the wind blew all afternoon and all that night. We settled down to endure it. We made a fire in the back of our shallow shelter and dried off a little. One of us watched it constantly. It was a little smoldering fire, but we kept potatoes cooking in the embers. We had pine kindling in one of the bags, and among us we had plenty of matches. There were broken branches and driftwood under the overhang of the bluff.

Roy was the first to watch the fire and he fell asleep. The fire was sputtering out when Mr. Allan noticed it. "Don't wake him," he said. "He looks exhausted. You all look beat up, if it comes to that. Stay where you are. I'll attend to it." He crawled back and coaxed up the fire.

We were all drowsy. I know I was sound asleep for a minute. I came to with a jerk. Everyone was settling down for the night under the tarpaulin. We were fairly well sheltered under the bluff. It was really cold, so we put on our sweaters. Bill had an extra one that his mother had made him bring, and he offered it to Mr. Allan, but Mr. Allan said he would be all right, so Bill put it on himself. We each had a blanket, but they were thin. Usually the nights were warm and we just used the blankets to cover the ground when we went to sleep. We kept one blanket by the fire for whoever was on watch.

When the wind shifted it would drive the rain in under the overhanging bluff and there would be puddles on the tarpaulin. The noise of the storm was like a roar. We would hear a crash now and then as if a tree had gone down, and then the woods groaned.

As tired as we were, we were too miserable to sleep, and, although we never would have admitted it, perhaps too frightened. I kept thinking how worried my family must be about me, and I was sure the others were thinking the same thing. We might have fallen asleep finally from sheer weariness, if Mr. Allan had not spoken.

Hurricane

To our astonishment Mr. Allan said, "I know you fellows think I'm not much of a guy, running out on you like that. Before any more times passes, I'd like to tell you all about it."

It was Terry's watch by the fire. "Come over here, Terry, and hear what I have to say." Mr. Allan raised his voice because of the storm. Terry wriggled across the sand to us. We sat up and listened.

"I knew that you would go over and find out that I had taken something out of the vault that you had discovered." Mr. Allan's voice was always rather deep and warm; now he sounded very grave. "Well, it was a chest. I thought from the way you described the place, especially because of the coat of arms, that it was something awfully important. Something I had been looking for."

Then he said he had not intended to do us out of the credit of finding it. He was just afraid that we would say something in East Edge before he had a chance to know for sure, and that the word would spread. It had to be protected. There was no time to lose. "I hope you understand?" he asked earnestly.

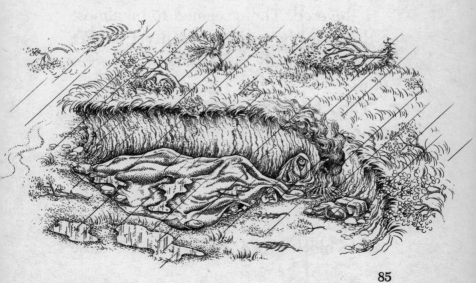

No one answered. Bill said after a pause, "*Was* it what you had been looking for?"

"No," answered Mr. Allan, "but it might have been a clue. Unfortunately, it was incomplete."

"What did the words mean that were cut in the stone under the coat of arms?" Terry asked.

"They were weathered, worn by wind and rain, but I finally made them out. 'My secret is mine.' "

Roy repeated the words.

I shivered. There seemed to be almost a threat in the words . . . and yet, hadn't the vault already given part of its secret to us?

Then Mr. Allan told us how he had gone over that very night with a block and tackle to move the slab. He had a time moving it. He hooked the tackle around a tree and got it off finally. When he tried to put it back on, the tackle block broke, so he couldn't close it. Then he said, "When I opened the chest, it was full of maps."

All during this time not one of us had said anything about the chest we had found. When Mr. Allan had seen that the chest he had found was not what he was looking for, why hadn't he come back and told us about it then?

The next thing he said surprised us. He had taken the chest to Santa Maria and put it in the bank for safekeeping! He had gone over the maps carefully, but he had discovered that every map needed another part to make it complete. No two maps joined. They were maps of some of our islands, but since the old Spanish names are not in use now, he could only tell which island was meant by what was left of the shape as each island was cut in half.

Anyhow he had not wasted any time. He had gone from island to island on the *Wandering Star* searching everywhere. If he could find the missing maps, he said, he was convinced that they would lead him to the thing he was looking for. But he had found nothing.

We could see that he had no inkling that we had them.

He thought there might be a clue somewhere in the old fort on Outer Island, because of the coat of arms over the door, but there was no way to get into the fort. He had tried many times since he came to East Edge.

"There must be another chest with the missing maps I need. I know it! It must be somewhere on these islands."

We didn't bat an eye. We were pretty proud of ourselves. We didn't look at each other. There was never a whisper. We had our secret. Since Mr. Allan had run out on us once, what was to prevent his taking the maps and disappearing for the second time? Perhaps the story about his taking the chest to the bank was made up.

We questioned him about what he

thought the maps might lead to, but he didn't give a straight answer. Then the storm grew so much worse that he may have thought that perhaps we would not all come through it. I know I was so cold and miserable that I thought I might really have the pneumonia that my family was always saying I was sure to get. Even under the tarpaulin I was damp. But I forgot the way I felt; I forgot the wind and the slashing rain when Mr. Allan broke the silence and told us that he was looking for a solid gold head of Alexander the Great.

Somewhere, he said, there was a golden head of Alexander that had been made for Lorenzo de' Medici at the end of the 15th century. It was an exact copy of a head of Greek marble which had been carved in Alexander's lifetime, a thousand years before. It was made by a Florentine goldsmith named Ugo Tucci.

At the great London Museum they

knew that the head had once existed. When he was a student, Mr. Allan had figured out where it might be. He had told the Museum about his theory. They had been interested, and he had worked with two of their top men, very learned they were. Following clues they had found in their research, they decided to have a look at the Spanish fortifications on Outer Island — especially because of the coat of arms above the entrance to the old ruin of a fort.

When Mr. Allan heard that they needed a teacher at East Edge, he applied for the job.

He went to the fort time and again, but found no way to get in. Some ancient calamity had tumbled the coquina walls of the ramparts so that the entrance was blocked. We knew those old stones. We played there many a time.

Mr. Allan went on to say that the head had later disappeared from the Medici collections. It might have been

sent to Spain when the first Cosimo de'
Medici married Eleanor of Toledo. Anyway, a century later the golden head
was rumored to be in the possession of
a Spanish nobleman. "Strange how these
things come about," Mr. Allan said.

This same nobleman was one of the
settlers of the new city of St. Augustine,
the first city in Florida. He brought
with him many possessions. It appears
that he had acted as temporary Governor of Florida for a short while. There
had been an uprising, perhaps an attack
by Indians, or by the French. The Governor and his followers had escaped to
one of the islands that the Spanish con-
trolled. It was this Governor's coat of
arms that had been cut into the coquina
slab. It was the same one that could be
seen, almost worn away, over the gates
of the fort.

He never became Governor again.
According to an old record, he died in
the islands after many hardships.

Mr. Allan believed that when the Governor ran away from St. Augustine, he had taken all his goods with him. Mr. Allan said that when he found where the Governor had hidden his possessions, we would find the head of gold.

"The head is priceless as a work of art," said Mr. Allan. He looked at each of us. "Don't you see that it must not be allowed to fall into the hands of people who will think of it only as gold?"

Then Bill remembered something. Had Mr. Allan seen the white ship? he asked. Did he know that a man named Da Costa was asking for him?

Mr. Allan appeared troubled. He said he had thought that was who it was. It had been another reason for him to stay on Center Island out of sight. If Da Costa found him he would be kidnapped and taken on that boat. They would try to make him tell what he knew about the head of Alexander.

The real owner of the ship was a private collector, one of the world's rich men, a very rich man indeed. He would stop at nothing to get what he wanted. And his mad ambition was to have the golden head for himself. Mr. Allan was just as determined to get it for the Museum, where all could admire it, and where it belonged.

We still didn't say a word about our maps, for we still were not completely sure of Mr. Allan, although we were liking him more and more, just the way we used to, and we all behaved as though he had never disappeared.

We sat in silence for a moment looking out into the turbulent darkness. There was the steady sound of the heavy rain under the wild howling of the wind. I remembered that violets grew in the woods around this spot in the spring. My mother loved violets and I used to gather them for her birthday in May. I don't know why I thought of it then, but I heartily wished myself at home!

"An interesting thing," said Mr. Allan thoughtfully. "One of the Czars is said to have made a wonderful collection of gold objects found near Tashkent and Samarkand, and along the route that Alexander took to India."

"How I'd like to see it!" Terry said.

"You know what I wonder," said Roy. "I wonder if there was an *original* gold head way back in the time of Alexander."

"By Jupiter, that's a big thought," exclaimed Mr. Allan. "I've tried to guess what the gold head might be, for we've really not much to go on, but I had not thought of that."

"Mr. Allan," Terry asked innocently, "speaking of museums . . . if you had a painting by one of those old painters you told us about, Velasquez, or somebody like that who lived in those days

94

. . . would you have something valuable? I mean, even a small painting?"

I held my breath. Surely Terry had gone too far!

Mr. Allan laughed. "You'd have something priceless."

We didn't say another word.

Bill asked suddenly, "Mr. Allan, what do you think would happen if that Da Costa and the people from the white ship found you?"

"They would do away with me in a minute after they had their information," said Mr. Allan.

"So what would you do if they caught up with you?"

A strange look came into Mr. Allan's face, a cold look, and yet a strong look. It scared me. I felt a chill along my spine.

"I'd do what any man would do, I'd defend myself," he answered. "To the death!"

I began to think about it.

What Happened at East Edge

The next morning I was awakened by the crash of a tree in the woods as it went down in the storm. The sounds of its fall, the tearing, breaking, crashing, seemed to merge into a savage scream. The others were awake too. We looked at each other with sudden understanding of the danger we were in. We stared at the storm — the pine trees twisting and turning, branches of trees and palmettos flying past us on the air. I watched three trees in the distance that seemed to be twisting in agony. Suddenly one of them popped out of the ground. It was a tremendous oak, but it was as though a giant hand had reached down and pulled it up, roots and all. Roots and all came up! I had never known a wind like it.

For breakfast we had potatoes again, washed down by rain water.

As the day wore on, we thought the storm was weaker. There was a lull, but I think we were passing through the eye of the storm, because after an hour or so, it struck again in fury.

Hours passed, but slowly the light changed, the rain stopped, the wind died down. We all wanted to try to head back to East Edge.

Mr. Allan said, "Let's leave the gear here. We'll have to figure some way to get across the sound. Perhaps make a raft. Better bring the ax and the ropes, and the tarp, I guess. Keep an eye out for a boat, just in case one has been cast on shore, but I'm afraid everything has been washed out to sea in the storm."

We took ropes and ax and tarpaulin

and climbed the ridge. It was south of where we usually camped, but we would get a good view from this point. Mr. Allan and Terry were ahead.

"Man, can he dish it out!" murmured Bill.

"Maybe it's easy, because it's the truth," I said.

"Could be," said Roy.

"What if he's not from the London Museum?" asked Bill in the same quiet voice.

We caught up with Terry and Mr. Allan and we all reached the top at the same time. We looked over toward Outer Island and East Edge. We looked, but there was no East Edge! We just stood there staring in horror.

Some of the docks were still there, but not many. There was just piling mostly. One part of a house — it looked like Bill's house — was still standing. It had been a two-story house, but only one part of the wall was there now, leaning over. Everything else was gone. The fishermen's shacks were a pile of boards. The sand dunes were gone or shifted around — even the sand dunes at the north end. The sea had eaten the shore back there. There was a big excavation in front of the Fort. The rocks had dropped away with the shifting sand. The Fort was all that was left on East Edge. A little rubble and heaped-up lumber. Everything else swept out to sea. It was a horrible sight — the bare beach, the bare land. A few gulls, back from wherever they had been, were flying in circles. I felt sick, and so weak I thought I might fall down. I don't remember when anyone of us spoke. It seemed a long, long time.

What a storm that had been! We hadn't realized that it was so bad. We could see the ocean clearly across the emptiness. It was calm now, with very small white breakers. It was low tide, far out.

Mr. Allan said, "Boys, I'm really sorry."

One of us said "thanks." And then it hit us. Everyone we knew was gone! Our parents, brothers, sisters, everyone we had known had disappeared. We couldn't take it in. I was shivering and I couldn't stop.

"What about the people who went off in that shrimp boat?" I asked. "We saw them get on. They must be somewhere."

"I hope so. I hope so," said Mr. Allan slowly. "With an ocean like that, who knows?"

"Yeah, a shrimp boat could be swamped in a sea like that," said Roy, and he began to cry.

"We must hope. We'll find out as soon as we can," Mr. Allan said. The sun had come out hot. He looked at us sadly. "We'll go to my camp. I have food there. That is, if nothing has happened to it. It's quite a way, on the south of the island." He headed in that direction.

We followed him, but none of us said a word during that walk, which was almost the length of Center Island.

I heard a bird's hoarse cry. A squirrel ran across a fallen tree. There was a line of terrapin sitting on a log near a swampy place. A frog jumped as I splashed by. The storm was over. Nature was in business once more. The world was coming back to life, but I knew that nothing would ever be the same again.

Mr. Allan had quite a snug camp, so hidden we could never have found it without him. A low, sturdy shack built of driftwood, with a small clearing in front of it, in the middle of very thick growth. It was that heavy growth of bushes and briars that had saved it from the wind. We stepped over a narrow brook, and as we came nearer to the shack, there was a spring. I drank a lot of it and splashed my face.

Mr. Allan had stored a lot of canned

goods. He made a fire and soon had a meal ready. There were beans and canned tuna, and he made hot tea. We did not feel like eating, but Mr. Allan had gone to so much trouble we tried to eat a little.

The air was full of many odors. It seemed as though I could smell the whole world at once. There was color too, from the yellow jessamine and other flowers scattered on the ground.

There were many fallen trees and enormous broken branches all through the island. The wind had really sailed through. I kept remembering the storm. Even when we saw the trees in the air, we hadn't realized what was happening. A hurricane that had taken everything from us. In my mind's eye I could see that oak tree rising out of the ground, but even then I had not understood the power of the wind, nor what it was doing at that moment at East Edge. Now I couldn't shut out from my mind all that I had seen in the last twenty-four hours: trees, branches, great palm leaves sailing through the air as though floating. I kept thinking of all the flotsam carried by the water ... some of it could have been part of my house.

Mr. Allan said we should scout around the island and see what we could see. He thought we might try to get over to Mr. Walker's place and see if it was still there. We must let them know that East Edge has disappeared. So we started out.

The Fight

We took our gear and the ropes. Mr. Allan added a can of food to each pack. He carried the tarpaulin and the ax. "Let's move on."

We reached the main trail that leads across the island. We were walking briskly. We looked behind us. Mr. Allan had not come out of the woods yet, but we saw two men from the white ship in the distance . . . the Mate and one of the crew. They were carrying guns and were still a fair way off.

We ran back into the woods and told Mr. Allan. We all ducked down, but we thought they might have seen us, so we scattered and disappeared into the trees. Mr. Allan was telling us to go this way, that way, to separate. He said we'd meet in a little pine wood just behind a sand dune on the west.

We found the pine wood and collected our thoughts. Mr. Allan said it would be safe for us to go on alone. He said he'd stay there. We said no, we'd get him over to Big Island. We suggested making a sled and using the tarpaulin to hide him. He didn't much want to do it, but anything was worth trying in a tight spot.

We worked fast. Mr. Allan used the ax and we had two hatchets. Terry and Roy worked at tying saplings together. We cut and stripped branches, and tied them up, but all the time we kept an eye out for trouble. We were afraid the noise would give us away but we had to risk it. We had a good view of any possible movement through the woods.

Our gear was piled under a tree, so

we left it there and put the ax with it. Mr. Allan got on the sled, his knees doubled up, and we covered him with the tarp. Using the rope, we set off to drag him to the landing. Three of us were in front, one in the rear. Off we went over the edge of the marsh toward the landing place for Big Island. We hoped to find some sort of boat washed up there or to catch one floating by. It was very boggy. The tide was coming in, but we slushed along as quickly as we could.

We were soon out of the marsh, but we hadn't reached good pulling ground yet when out of the woods about a hundred yards away came the Mate and the crewman.

They yelled at us, "Where are you going?"

We didn't answer. We went on faster. Mr. Allan was well covered up, so there seemed to be only four of us. I was sorry for Mr. Allan bumping along like that. We reached the road that led to the landing, but they were gaining.

One of the men shouted, "Wait a minute!"

Looking over my shoulder, I saw the sailor aiming his gun. I think it was mostly to scare us. I said so. "He won't shoot," I said.

Mr. Allan spoke then in a muffled voice. We didn't dare stop. Then he said more loudly, "Fellows, I want you to leave me. You'd better run. I'll be all right. I'll try to meet you at the wharf. Look for a boat."

"We can't leave you," one of us said. "Those men are armed."

"You've nothing to do with them. They're after me. Beat it! That's an order."

We jumped off the path and darted among the trees, leaving the sled there with its curious looking bundle.

Seeing us running, one man called, "Hey, wait! We must talk to you." When we didn't stop they paused to parley, and then came on. The sailor fired, but the shot went wild.

We were hidden by the trees and underbrush, so we hung about for a bit, watching. We wondered what they were up to, and we were frightened for Mr. Allan.

The men seemed to be curious about what we had been dragging on the sled. The Mate even had his hand outstretched to uncover it.

As they came up to it, Mr. Allan, who must have been watching their approach from under a corner of the tarpaulin, flung it off with a wild whoop, jumped up, and rushed at them.

They stood still in fright for a second. The sailor stepped back with an expression on his face of a man who has walked into a trap.

Mr. Allan slugged the Mate, but the sailor, having recovered from his surprise, now tackled Mr. Allan. Mr. Allan gave a good account of himself, but two strong seamen were too much for him. Besides, the ground was slippery from the rain, and his feet slid in the wet sand. He almost lost his balance, and in that second the sailor had pinned down his arms. Now the two men were pulling and pushing him into the water. I suppose they had left the sea skiff somewhere near.

This was too much for us. We looked at each other and made a signal to Roy, who was peering around a tree a few feet away. With a rush we joined the fighting.

Mr. Allan saw us coming. He freed himself and struck out again. Bill charged the sailor, whose back was toward him, and pulled up his leg so that he fell down. Bill nearly went down too. Terry and I went for the Mate, who had a stranglehold on Mr. Allan. The sailor was up again hitting Mr. Allan from the rear. Roy did some kicking

and pulling. I hung on the Mate's arm
and he let Mr. Allan go. He swung at
me, but I ducked and butted him in the
midriff. Mr. Allan swung with his right
and the Mate went down.

It took three of us to put down the
sailor, but this time he lost his wind and
we pushed him into the ditch. We could
hear him swearing.

"Run for it now, boys!" gasped Mr.

Allan. "Come on, we'll try to make the wharf. We'll swim across if all else fails." He stopped a moment only to be sure that we were with him. This time we ran without looking back. I guess none of us thought of their guns. The two men had tossed them aside when they slugged it out with Mr. Allan. But I remembered their rifles when a bullet whizzed over my head.

I glanced back. Both men were up now and coming after us. They were too far away for me to see their faces, but I could feel their anger.

We jumped down into the ditch alongside the path and ran low. There was a little water in the ditch, but it was draining off.

Both men fired now, one right after the other. I wondered if they were firing to frighten us or to call others to help them.

We ran as fast as we could. We were

coming to the landing place for Big Island. We didn't know how we could get across the inlet when we reached it, but we kept running. Roy seemed to read my thought. "We'll swim across," he said.

They fired again, and Bill, who was behind me, said, "That almost got me. I could hear it whistle by my head."

We bent lower now, but finally we made it. We scrambled up onto the landing just as Mr. Walker and his three sons arrived at their boat dock on the other side. We dashed down the dock until we were almost opposite to where they were. It wasn't far across the water, and as we ran Mr. Walker called, "What's the trouble?"

Mr. Allan shouted, "Some men are trying to shoot us!"

Mr. Walker raised the gun he always had with him and sent a shot across the water. He was aiming high, but he shot as if he meant business. We were at the dock's edge by now, and we turned and saw the men come up short as the shot rang out.

Slim and one of the other boys were down in the water turning up the boats. They said afterwards they had come down to see what damage had been done by the hurricane . . . lucky for us.

One of their boats had been carried out to sea, but it was only a minute before they had a boat righted. The other son, Jerome was his name, ran to help. They tipped the water out of the boat and pushed it to the dock. Mr. Walker stepped in. Slim and one son got in too, and they had some poles or paddles, I'm not sure which. They had an oar from somewhere. Anyway, Mr. Walker was standing up in the center as they sculled across. The oldest boy stayed behind working on the boats.

The men had stopped at the first shot. Now they started after us again. Mr. Walker let out another shot. The Mate and his partner didn't fire back. I guess they knew better. Mr. Walker wasn't trying to hit them. He could have done that easily enough. But the men were still coming.

The boys landed the boat just as the two men walked up. The sailor had a black eye.

"O.K.," said the Mate. "O.K., Traherne."

We said, "That's Mr. Allan. You've made a mistake."

The Mate said, "We know. It's Mr. Allan Traherne. We are taking him in."

Mr. Walker said, "What kind of law are you fellows, just walking up?"

The Mate said, "We'll take him quietly. We'll turn him over to the sheriff. He's wanted."

Mr. Allan said, "They haven't anything on me. They just want to get me on their ship."

"Hold it. Hold it," said Mr. Walker. His gun was cradled in the crook of his arm. A big man. A formidable figure of authority and purpose. "Slim, take their guns," he said.

"What *is* this?" asked the Mate. He and the sailor looked at Mr. Walker and his sons. They looked at Mr. Allan, whose days of exposure had made him stronger and tougher, and they looked at the four of us. They handed over their guns.

"The first thing I want to know," said Mr. Walker to us, "is how did East Edge make out?"

We didn't answer, but Bill put his head down as if he were starting to cry. Mr. Allan spoke, "It was wiped out."

Mr. Walker exclaimed, "Oh, Lord, that's terrible!" He looked away over the water for a minute, then turned back to Mr. Allan. "Now, let me understand, what was it you said about these men?"

But Mr. Allan was not thinking about himself. The big thing was that East Edge was gone. "Yes, dreadful. There's nothing left. You didn't hear anything, Mr. Walker?"

"Not a word. Not a word."

"The boys saw some people getting on a shrimp boat before the storm struck," Mr. Allan told him. Mr. Walker shook his head, but said nothing more.

Then Mr. Allan seemed to shake himself a little. A sharp, angry gleam came into his blue eyes. His voice was strong. "These men," he said, "are off a foreign ship. They don't intend to turn me over to the law. They have come to kidnap me. They think I know about an archeological find . . . it's a piece of sculpture. I have no idea where it is, but they want to know everything I know. They would think nothing of killing me to get what they are after."

"They're thugs!" exclaimed Slim, delighted.

Mr. Walker turned and called to his son on the dock across the water, "Bring another rowboat."

The boy nodded and climbed down into the boat he had just bailed out and rowed over to us. We waited in silence, watching. Slim stood near us, his mouth half open, and his eyes shining. The Mate and the sailor did not seem to know what to say or do. They had never seen people behave like this!

"We had better go over to my island and settle this," said Mr. Walker.

Who Was Mr. Allan?

Climb in, climb in," ordered Mr. Walker, so we slid into the boats. Mr. Walker had taken charge. The Mate and the sailor seemed in a daze. They sat stiff and unsmiling, the sailor with a sullen frown. They never took their angry eyes off Mr. Walker. Once they whispered together for a minute. They seemed to be plotting some mischief. I felt the way I feel when I run into an alligator unexpectedly . . . you never know what may happen.

When we reached the other side of

the creek, we saw the horse and wagon
a few yards away and the three saddle
horses hitched nearby. We all got out of
the boats and turned to watch two men
who were riding handsome horses along
the creek pathway. They were within
hailing distance and they galloped up
when they saw us.

"Howdy, Marshall," we called. One of
the men waved to us. They were both
neighbors of the Walkers. Big men they
were, with an ease of manner that

showed they felt equal to any situation.

"Howdy, Judge Henry. Howdy, Marshall," said Mr. Walker.

Marshall wore a black hat and a cape that flowed over his saddle and gave him the air of someone in a storybook. Judge Henry sat very straight in the saddle. He always looked to me like pictures of Abraham Lincoln. He had a stern face. He wasn't really a judge. His name was Henry Judge, but everybody called him Judge Henry. He was well liked and settled many an argument just by common sense.

"How did things go over your way? Was there much damage?" asked Mr. Walker.

"No, we got off lightly. We just came to see if help was needed here."

"There's bad news from East Edge," Mr. Walker told them. "Come up to the house and we will see what's to be done. I'll send a couple of men at once to row over and see what the situation is. . . .

But just at this moment there is trouble with these two men. I'd like to sift it to the bottom. Maybe you two can give us a little help."

The Mate gave a swift glance at the two big men who had joined us. Then he spoke to Mr. Walker. He took a step forward and spoke in a formal manner. "Permit me, sir, to confess that we have made a mistake. This gentleman is not the man we are after. I shall so inform the Captain." He turned to Mr. Allan and said, as if to a stranger, "My apologies, sir."

Mr. Allan bowed slightly in acknowledgement. He tried to hide a smile.

The Mate turned back to Mr. Walker. "With your permission, sir, we will get back to the ship, as we are under orders to sail at dawn."

"Just a minute," said Mr. Walker. He turned to Mr. Allan. "Shall I let them go?"

Mr. Allan said he had no charges to

prefer against them. He said they had not done anything wrong. They were just trying to catch him and they hadn't caught him.

Judge Henry looked grave and said something I didn't hear, but it seemed to startle the men from the ship.

"Slim, row them over," said Mr. Walker, "and give them their guns when you get to the other side." Slim and the two men stepped into the rowboat, but the sailor did the rowing across. I suppose he felt it was the least he could do.

Mr. Walker was still running things. He mounted his horse and his sons mounted theirs and they rode off at a slow pace with Marshall and Judge Henry.

Slim was back to drive us in the wagon before they were out of sight.

As we turned into the yard we saw a man on a barn-colored horse riding up to the house. It looked like Mr. Parker.

It *was* Mr. Parker! We scrambled down and ran to him. "Mr. Parker! Mr. Parker!" we shouted. He flung the reins over the horse's head to the ground and ran to meet us. He was as astonished as we were. "Boys, is it really you? Roy, Terry, Larry, Bill, I can hardly believe my eyes. Let me look at you. It's good to see you. We thought you were lost in the storm . . . the only ones lost."

"The only ones! Do you mean our people are safe? That everyone from East Edge is all right?" We could scarcely speak in our excitement.

"Yes, all are safe . . . all of us. How happy they will be to see you. We saw it was going to be a whopper and we got out just in time in the fishing boats. We are now on the other side of Big Island in Inland Harbor. Some of the fishermen are putting us up in their houses."

Mr. Walker and the two men had

joined us. Mr. Walker said, "This is great news, great news."

Mr. Allan came over, followed by Slim. "Hello, Mr. Parker."

Mr. Parker took one startled look at the bearded man in the battered clothes. "Allan!" he exclaimed. "This is a day of miracles."

"It is for all of us."

"So it's you. I don't believe I should have known you."

Then everyone began asking questions at once. Mr. Parker turned to us. "Do you know if East Edge came through all right?"

We could not say it. Finally, "Everything was . . . was . . ." Bill said. "From what we saw from the ridge on Center Island . . . it was pretty bad . . ."

"Don't be afraid to tell me," said Mr. Parker. "There was a lot of damage?"

"It was total. There was nothing left," said Mr. Walker.

Mr. Parker said nothing. He looked

off into the woods beyond. His face seemed old and very sad.

"From the ridge," said Mr. Allan gently, "there seemed to be nothing standing. All had been swept out to sea."

"Some of our men have gone around in a fishing boat to see what happened," said Mr. Parker. "I came this way to see how the Walkers and the rest of Big Island came through."

"We'll say good-bye now," one of us said to Mr. Walker. "And thank you for coming to our rescue."

Then as we all began to thank him and were ready to start off to walk to the fishing village to see our folks, Mr. Walker raised his hands. "Wait a minute, boys. It's twelve miles. Slim will take you in the wagon."

"A wagon couldn't get through," Mr. Parker told him. "There are trees down across the road in several places, and there is a bad wash-out a few miles from here."

"I'll send Walter over to tell them you're safe and find out what we can send to help out ... blankets ... food ... whatever they need. Meanwhile there's food ready here, so all come and eat." He went off to find his son.

"We'll get together and clear the road in no time," said Marshall. "You can go the first thing in the morning."

"Walter will tell them you're safe," said Mr. Parker, as Walter rode off. "Your parents are fine. Your sisters and your brothers and your friends are all fine. We had a bad time, but it is over. They have been mighty worried about you. They all have. You should have heard Nan talking about her brother Roy." He put his arm around the shoulder of the boy next to him.

Mr. Walker came back. "We had quite a little skirmish down the creek," he told Mr. Parker.

"There were two sorry looking men

when George Walker finished with them," said Judge Henry.

"You must get Allan to tell you the whole story one day." He turned to Mr. Allan. "What I'd like to know is something more about this sculpture they were so interested in."

"It's a long, long story," said Mr. Allan. "But I'd like to tell it when you have time."

"What about that chest you hauled into Santa Maria?" asked Mr. Walker.

We looked at each other. So that part of the story was true anyway.

"I didn't know anyone knew that!" replied Mr. Allan.

"Well, I knew it. I am one of the directors of the bank."

Mr. Allan told him that the chest had contained maps. He repeated what he had told us, that the maps were not whole but only parts of maps, quite useless without the missing parts. "I think if I had the other sections, I should find clues to the place where the sculpture is hidden . . . the sculptured head they were talking about."

Everything he said fitted in. One of us nodded slowly. I knew they all felt as I did, that the time had come to tell him that we had the maps, but we knew that we couldn't speak in front of the others.

"As soon as I can get away, I'll take back these partial maps to my sponsors in London," Mr. Allan was saying, "but there is really not enough to go on, and nothing to come back for."

Mr. Parker suddenly exclaimed, "Allan, in all the trouble, I forgot that I had a letter about you. It came in the last mail."

Mr. Allan looked bewildered. Mr. Parker explained, "When you disappeared, I copied the address off of one of the long envelopes you get every week. (There were a couple of letters in your box.) I wrote to England, and I had a letter back the other day from the London Museum thanking me ... saying you are a very distinguished ... what was the word? ... on a mission here from the Museum."

"Yes, a mission to search for the sculpture," said Mr. Allan.

"Anyway," continued Mr. Parker, "they want to be told as soon as I have news of you. Wait a minute! I must have that letter here ... I put it in my pocket ..." He began to look for it and brought out a long envelope and handed it to Mr. Walker.

Mr. Walker read it. "So you are Mr. Allan Traherne, a distinguished archeologist," he said.

"That's the word," said Mr. Parker.

"A very impressive letter." Mr. Walker gave it to Mr. Allan. "They seem to think you are a great man," he said to

Mr. Allan, "but of course we all think that around here anyway. Now, will everyone please come and eat?"

Mr. Allan said that he felt so grimy he'd like to wash up and headed for the rear of the Walkers' house.

We looked at each other. We felt that the time had come to let Mr. Allan in on what we knew that he didn't. We caught up with him at some distance from the others.

One of us asked him in a low voice if we could talk to him for a minute.

He stopped. "Certainly," he answered. He also spoke in a low voice, as though he could tell that this was something serious.

Then one at a time all four of us told him our great secret.

We asked him if he remembered telling us that if we ever found anything old and buried, not to stop there at that one thing but always to dig deeper?

He didn't take another step. He bent closer to us and asked in a low voice, "Yes. And then what did you do?"

"We dug deeper," we all said.

"Where?" he asked. "Where?"

At the place of the vault there was another vault below the vault he had seen. His face was white, his eyes dark with excitement. Then we went on telling him that when we got into the lower vault we found a chest. Mr. Allan wanted to know if we had left it there.

"Oh, no," we answered, "we moved it."

Our voices had been dropping lower and lower, and now Mr. Allan almost whispered, "What did you say?"

"No," Bill said. "We moved the chest to a cave on the north side of Center Island and we buried it in an oil drum."

Then he wanted to know if we had tried to open it.

We told him everything exactly as it happened. Each of us came up with a bit of information, whenever Mr. Allan or any one of us paused for breath. We told him about the pieces of maps and how they were wrapped in oilskin. He said it was the same in the chest he had at Santa Maria.

"Boys," he said quietly, "this is such great news!"

Then Roy said in almost a whisper, "That's not all that was in the chest."

"Oh," exclaimed Mr. Allan. "What else?"

Then we told him there was just one other thing in the chest and that was a painting . . . a picture of a head such as Mr. Allan himself had described as sculptured in gold. In the picture it was a yellow color with several glinting and glittering spots on it.

"That's it. That's it," he said. He looked at us and said solemnly, "You — Bill, Terry, Roy, and Larry — you four have no doubt solved the whole thing.

By finding the first chest, then the great, clever way you went about finding the second chest. I'm sure it won't be long before we discover the head with such clues as you four have unearthed." He went on. "And you four will get, and deserve, I promise you, a tremendous monetary reward from the London Museum. Finding this head has been one of its main projects for a long, long time."

Terry looked around to make sure that no one had come near to our huddle. There was no one. By now everyone else was busy eating. Terry said, "I've been thinking that maybe it was a trick."

We were startled. He explained. "Maybe whoever buried the two vaults with the chests, one on top of another, wanted whoever discovered the maps to be misled. They would rush off chasing clues and wandering around all the islands hereabout, trying to locate spots as markers to connect with other spots that would finally point to the main . . . the hidden location. What if it all led back to the original place? You know, the high ridge at the site where we found the maps is nice and dry. It would be a long way down to dig until you'd hit ground water level."

Mr. Allan was smiling. "Anyway, it's an awfully good spot to start digging."

The Head

Mr. Walker and the others were off clearing the road to the fishing village. They said we were not needed, so we went back to Center Island with Mr. Allan. We made our way to the campsite on the ridge. Only our determination to get there made us keep on.

At first the trail — the dirt road used by Mr. Walker — was clear. Then we came to an oak tree that had been struck by lightning. It hung over the road. The branches blocked the way to any wagons, and it was hardly possible for those on foot to get by the great branches and the webs of moss.

We were carrying a block and tackle, shovels, an ax, and ropes that we had borrowed from the barn. We passed these from one to the other as we pushed and cut our way through.

Finally we reached the path that we had made over the dunes and through the woods to the top. There it was even worse. The climb, not more than twenty feet, was a tangle of vines, leaves, brambles, moss, palmettos, and fallen branches. It was easy to guess that the vault had once been buried and had been uncovered by some long forgotten wind and then covered again for a hundred years, perhaps, by the creeping growth.

There was a tree down there too, and sand from a dune had blown across the path. We had to crawl around it.

When we reached the vault we found that all the branches and brambles we had heaped there to hide it had blown away in the storm. The stones we had moved away were still lying on all sides near the trees and the open vault itself was full of water. So was the top vault still tilted just off of it.

We stood there wondering what to do. Mr. Allen admired the way we had gotten into it. He examined everything. The rain had washed away almost all the sandy earth from the lowest side of the vault where it opened on the slope. It was easy to get at it, too. A few minutes digging there and we would soon see if there were another vault under this one. The same thought occurred to all of us, even before Mr. Allan spoke. Only two could get down in that space. Terry helped Mr. Allan, and we cleared away the dirt as they threw it out. It was only a few minutes before they reached the bottom of the stones.

They kept on digging. We watched, scarcely breathing. There was nothing below. Certainly not another vault. Mr. Allan leaned on his shovel, but Terry kept making the hole larger. It was his idea. He hated to give it up, I think.

"There's a wooden piling here at the corner," he said.

Mr. Allan looked at it, knocked on it with his shovel. The vault rested on a sort of wooden post. Mr. Allan cleaned it off, took a knife from his pocket, and scratched a spot on the side. "It's cypress," he said. He began to dig around it. We took out shovels and made a way to the upper corner. We all dug furiously, widening the open hole, making it easier to dig under the vault.

"Larry's found another post," said Roy. Sure enough, I had uncovered another six-inch upright log upon which the vault rested.

"We can be sure there are two more under the opposite corners," said Mr. Allan. "They were put here to keep the vaults from sinking too deeply into the earth and being lost forever."

Terry was excavating under the vault.

The posts did indeed keep the vaults on even keel. We, too, were helping dig.

"What is this?" asked Terry in a voice trembling with strain. He had hit a curious layer of small stones and pebbles mixed with a few shells. It poured out into the newly dug area. A second later we came to it too.

"Go slow," said Mr. Allan. "There may be something there." He put his head and shoulders under and moved the pebbles with his hands. We heard a startled gasp, almost a groan. He slid back out with something in his hands.

We stared. It was the skull of a small animal, a possum it may have been, by the look of that ugly, pointed nose.

"It is meant for a warning," said Mr. Allan. "A skull says *death*. It was no accident that put it there." He laid it on the edge of the dig.

We looked at each other with hope. It was strange. The skull had been put there to scare people, but it was doing just the opposite to us. Instead of telling us we were on the wrong track, it was a sign that maybe we were right.

Mr. Allan went under once more. He pushed a little farther in. Showers of pebbles rolled out on each side. "Take this, Terry," he called in a muffled voice. He pushed and pulled a black box toward us. Terry reached in and, although it was difficult, pulled it the rest of the way out. Mr. Allan slipped back and stood up. Terry and Mr. Allan lifted the square box which was very heavy for its size, and Mr. Allan held it and stepped out of the hole at the open end. We followed.

We walked the few yards to our campsite where there was a cleared space, and stood around him looking at the box. It was made of lead and seemed to be welded together on every side. He put it down on the ground and sat down. We sat in a circle around him.

"The question now is, how do we get

into it?" said Mr. Allan.

"I think I'll make a fire," said Bill, springing up to gather wood. Roy and I helped him. The ground was already dry on the ridge. The sandy soil and the pitch of the land had drained it off quickly, and the sun was hot, but dry wood was another matter. Still, we had a pile of driftwood that we had gathered from time to time stored in a scooped-out place that was pretty dry. Bill is a good firemaker. We cut up some splinters with the ax, and in less than ten minutes we had a fire going.

Terry and Mr. Allan were still looking at the box.

"Do you think it can be in there?" I asked.

"We shall see. We shall see," said Mr. Allan. "But what is the best and safest way to open it?"

Bill and Roy sat down now.

"We might use a can opener," said Roy carelessly.

Mr. Allan stared at him. "We might," he said.

"Where is that bag of food we left here?" asked Terry.

We all jumped up and rushed to look. It was under the tree where we had put it. The canvas bag was soaked, but we shook it and opened it.

"There's a can opener in here." It was almost a whisper. Bill found it and handed it to Mr. Allan. It was a strong one. As we went back to the box and the fire, I hoped it was strong enough.

Mr. Allan examined the box. We stood around him hoping to be useful. "I believe this seam may be weak," he said. He managed to insert the sharp point of the cutter. He pushed. It moved. It was not hard to cut through the lead. Carefully, carefully, one side was done. Now another side, more slowly. He pushed back some flimsy stuff that was in the box. Half of the box could now be bent back. He cut a little

more along a third side. We stared at the silk cloths that spilled out of the box.

Mr. Allan lifted out the head. The shape even in the wrapping was unmistakable. He held it for a moment as if it were a new baby. He stood up.

"It's heavy," he said. "Help me. This is it."

Our hands went out to help him support it, as he unwrapped the dark cloth from around it.

"Good heavens," he said. "Good heavens, it's perfect!"

The sun shone on the heavy object in

his hands. So bright. I had thought I knew what it would be like from the painting, but it was so much more than we had expected. I suppose we had thought it would be old and dulled by the hundreds of years it had been under the earth, but this was new and alive and shining. We hadn't expected that, nor the weight of it.

No one spoke. This was happening to us. We would never forget how we stood — friends together — on that quiet ridge top. I remember the color of the sky. There were no clouds, the breeze was fresh and sweet. We could smell the woods, and there the five of us stood with the golden head of Alexander sparkling in our hands.